Look, this is my little friend Fifi.
We love to play together.

One, two, will you come
cuddle up and have some fun?

Three, four, have a look
sit with me and read this book!

First published in Belgium and Holland by Clavis Uitgeverij, Hasselt – Amsterdam, 2015
Copyright © 2015, Clavis Uitgeverij

English translation from the Dutch by Clavis Publishing Inc. New York
Copyright © 2016 for the English language edition: Clavis Publishing Inc. New York

Visit us on the web at www.clavisbooks.com

Little Billy-Bob Eats It All Up written and illustrated by Pauline Oud
Original title: *Kleine Billy-Bob eet alles op*
Translated from the Dutch by Clavis Publishing

ISBN 978-1-60537-296-9

This book was printed in July 2016 at CP Printing (Heyuan) Limited,
Heyuan Hi-Tech Development Zone, Heyuan, Guangdong Province,
P.R.C. Postal Code: 517000, China

First Edition
10 9 8 7 6 5 4 3 2 1

Little
Billy-Bob
Pauline Oud

Eats It All Up

Clavis

NEW YORK

Grumble, grumble!
What do I hear?
Fifi's stomach
is acting weird.

Do you see their empty tummies too?
Do you think they should eat something?

And **Billy-Bob**'s tummy?
It won't stop grumbling either!

Yummy, delicious food. Nom, nom, nom!
Fifi eats her little plate of porridge all by herself.

And little **Billy-Bob**?
He ate his porridge all **UP**!

Look, the cat would like something to eat too. What do you think? Can he have some porridge too?

Before they go outside,
Fifi eats a tasty banana.

And little Billy-Bob?
He ate his banana all UP!

Does the banana peel belong in your pocket or in the garbage can?

Fifi takes a green apple
to eat along the way.

Yummy, that looks good!?
Do you like fruit too?

And little **Billy-Bob**?
He ate his apple all UP!

Look at that, well done!
Fifi is drinking without a bib.

And little **Billy-Bob**?
He drank his water all **UP**!

Can you drink from a cup?
While wearing a bib of course!

And little **Billy-Bob**?
He ate his toast all **UP**!

After playing, Fifi happily
eats carrots with a hard-boiled egg.

What are you eating today?
What do you really like to eat?

And little **Billy-Bob**?
He ate his all UP!

Ssssh, listen! What do I hear?
The tummies have stopped their funny grumbling.

Hey, what do I see?
Is your tummy nice and round too?

Both little bellies are all full now.
Good food! Their tummies are nice and round!

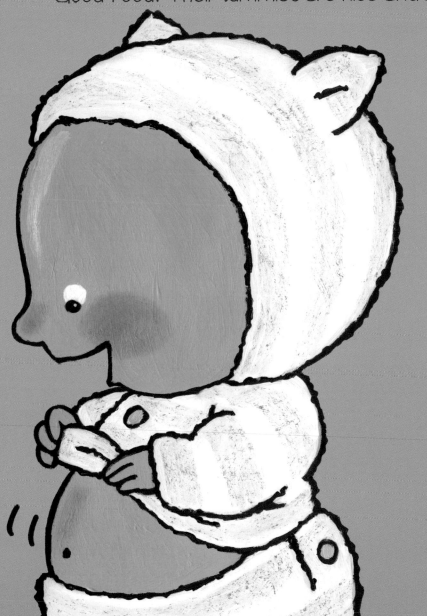

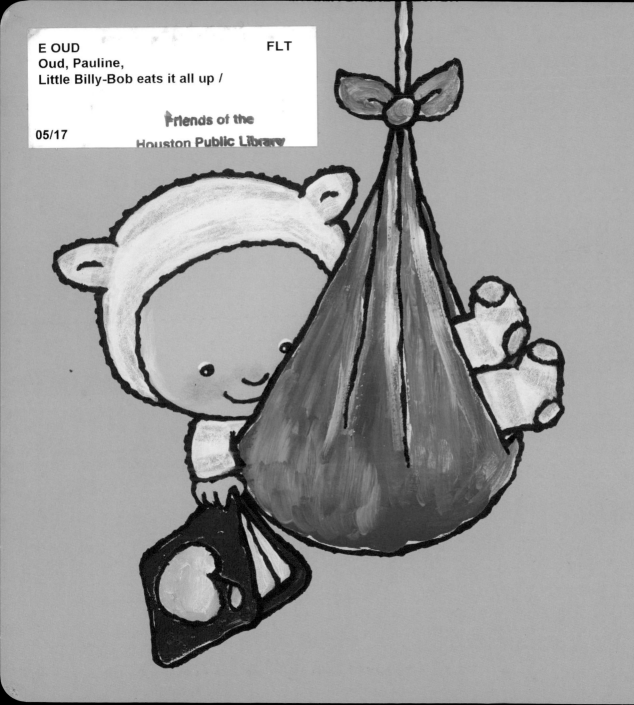